amoeba aardvark

bat

hedgehog shark slug

olar bear

pig

dolphin

moose

uffin

dog

snail

ck billed platypus spider armadillo

To Jake
love, Mummy
KD

Karen Duncan, Samantha Stringle, Jackie Robb, and Berny Stringle
assert their moral right to be identified as the authors of this work.

First published in the United States in 1997 by Price Stern Sloan, Inc.
A member of The Putnam & Grosset Group,
New York, New York.

First published in the United Kingdom by David Bennett Books Ltd.

ISBN 0-8431-7931-7

First Edition
1 3 5 7 9 10 8 6 4 2

Library of Congress Catalog Number: 96-69524

Production by Imago
Printed in Singapore

Created by bang on the door™

Illustrated by
Karen Duncan and Samantha Stringle

Story by
Jackie Robb and Berny Stringle

PRICE STERN SLOAN
Los Angeles

Slug was very greedy
he really loved to eat,

He munched on leaves and weeds
and grass... but
ettuce was his treat.

Slug really needed glasses
'cause he always had to chew

On anything he came across
with a vaguely greenish hue.

He bit clean through a garden hose
and caused an awful flood,

But Slug was in slug heaven
'cause slugs are into mud.

He chomped on green galoshes
the smell was really icky,

It took him weeks of bathing
to wash away the sticky!

Slug was beaten by Stick Insect
when he nibbled on its head

And kicked out of the garden
when he tried Frog's leg instead.

Slug guzzled half the fishpond
as the sun shone on the slime

t turned a tasty shade of green
nd fooled him every time.

Slug slipped into a kitchen
unnoticed and unseen,

nd took a bite of everything
at looked remotely green.

A small girl yelled out, "Mommy!. What's that creeping on our food

he didn't know that slug
as just a hungry little dude.

She put slug in the dustbin
with the slop food for the pigs,

He rummaged 'round 'til he found
Some apples and old figs.

The bin was taken to a farm
an angry pig cried, "ugh!

Look what's in our dinner,
it's that greedy little slug!"

The farmer said, "I'll hire him,
There's greenfly on my beans.

So Slug ate every single fly
until the beans were clean.

The ending to this story
might sound a little funny

But Slug was paid in dollars
and he promptly ate the money.

bee
elephant
rabbit
kangaroo
bear
hippo
squid
plankton
zebra
bug
whale
pea brain
worm
horse
brai
ce
jellyfish
sheep
penguin
rat
crab